To my mom, who is the very definition of happy
—H.K.

For Richard, for always
—S.M.

ISBN 978-0-06-288789-4 (trade bdg.) — ISBN 978-0-06-293103-0 (special edition)

The artist used Adobe Photoshop to create the digital illustrations for this book.
Typography by Chelsea C. Donaldson
19 20 21 22 23 PC 10 9 8 7 6 5 4 3 2 1 ❖ First Edition

You Are My Happy

Hoda Kotb

pictures by Suzie Mason

HARPER

An Imprint of HarperCollins Publishers

The night is near, today is done.
It's time for bed, my fuzzy one.

Let's cuddle up, one kiss, one hug.
Let's settle down, my snuggle bug.

What made us happy all day through?
Let's count those things, just me and you.

For babies bursting out of eggs,

for standing up on wobbly legs.

For growing tall, for lucky breaks,

and even learning from mistakes.

That's what
made me happy.

For special friends who made me giggle
and silly songs that made me wiggle.

For space to play, for shade to rest,
for secret spots we love the best.

That's what
made me happy.

For being brave, for brand-new wings,
for the joy that flying brings.

For splashes together in the lake,
for cozy nests our mamas make.

That's what
made me happy.

For twinkling lights that say good night,
for nestling babies cuddled tight.

Every night and all day through,
the one I'm thankful for is you.

You are my happy.